BOOK ANALYSIS

Written by Lauri[illegible] Sable
Translated by Sol[illegible]rlodot

[illegible]he Litt[illegible] Chinese Seamstress

BY DAI SIJIE

BrightSummaries.com

DAI SIJIE

CHINESE NOVELIST AND FILMMAKER WRITING IN FRENCH

- **Born in the province of Fujian (China) in 1954**
- **Notable works:**
  - *Balzac and the Little Chinese Seamstress* (2000), novel
  - *Mr. Muo's Travelling Couch* (2003), novel
  - *The Chinese Botanist's Daughters* (2006), film

Born in China in 1954, Dai Sije is a writer and filmmaker who has lived in France since 1984. At 22 years old, at the end of the Cultural Revolution, he enrolled at the University of Pekin where he studied History of Art. Having received a scholarship, he chose to continue his studies in France, at the Institut des hautes études cinématographiques in Paris. He was awarded the Jean Vigo prize for his first long film, *China, My Sorrow* (1989). His film *The Chinese Botanist's Daughters* (2006) was also met with acclaim from the cinema critics.

Balzac and the Little Chinese Seamstress (2000) is his debut novel. In 2003, he was awarded the Femina Prize for his story *Mr. Muo's Travelling Couch* , which was later followed by *Par une nuit où la lune ne s'est pas levee* (*Once on a Moonless Night*, 2007) and *L'acrobatie aérienne de Confucius* (2009).

BALZAC AND THE LITTLE CHINESE SEAMSTRESS

A NOVEL AT THE HEART OF THE CHINESE CULTURAL REVOLUTION

- **Genre:** novel
- **Reference edition:** Sije, D. (2002) *Balzac and the Little Chinese Seamstress*. London: Vintage Books.
- **First edition:** 2000
- **Themes:** Chinese Cultural Revolution, rehabilitation, reading, love, communism

Balzac and the Little Chinese Seamstress (2000) is Dai Sije's Masterpiece. The author received no less than three awards for it (*Edmée de La Rochefoucauld, Relay du Roman d'évasions* and *Roland de Jouvenel*).

During the Cultural Revolution (1966-1976), Sije's parents were imprisoned and the adolescent was sent to the mountains to a rehabilitation camp. This experience inspired him to write the story of his two protagonists, who are young intellectuals sent to a small village on the mountain called the "Phoenix of the Sky", to be re-educated by peasants. There, the young men discover Western books and meet the Little Seamstress.

A filmmaker, Sije adapted the novel for the screen. The resulting film (which bears the same name) was presented at the Cannes Film Festival in 2002 as part of the "Uncertain Regard" selection.

SUMMARY

The story opens on an evening of the year 1971 in a small village on the mountain called the "Phoenix of the Sky". The narrator and his friend Luo have been sent there, along with many other young intellectuals, in order to be re-educated by the poor peasants, according to a rule set up by the communist regime. Because they are also the sons of educated people, their re-education is probably never going to end, while for others it usually lasts about two years.

Several months after their arrival, they meet the daughter of the local tailor, and nickname her "the Little Seamstress". They are nearly the same age and immediately become friends; the narrator even suspects that his friend has fallen in love with her, but Luo states that she is not civilized enough for him.

Soon after this encounter, the young woman writes to Luo to invite the two young men to give her village a show of "oral cinema", which is their specialty. As they arrive, Luo is suffering from a severe malaria crisis, and the young woman stays up all night to care for him. In the darkness, the narrator believes he saw her kiss him.

On the way back, the two protagonists stop at the village of Four-Eyes, who is also being re-educated. As he is looking for a sweater in Four-Eyes' room, the narrator discovers a bag locked up with a key under his bed. The narrator and Luo question him about its contents, because they are convinced, and rightly so, that it must be filled with books that have been forbidden by the regime (in China, all the Oriental books are forbidden because they are judged to be dangerous), which Four-Eyes denies.

In spring, Four-Eyes is forced to accept the help of his two friends in order to accomplish a task that his own short-sightedness prevents him from doing, in exchange for one of the books hidden in his bag: *Ursule Mirouët* (1841) by Balzac (French writer, 1799-1850). The narrator and Luo, who have never had an opportunity to read Western works, devour the novel with fascination and enthusiasm. As soon as he is done reading, Luo goes to the Little Seamstress. When he comes back, he tells the narrator how they made love for the first time.

The two friends try to obtain more books from Four-Eyes, but to no avail.

In summer, an opportunity presents itself: Four-Eyes must collect authentic songs from the mountains destined to be published in an official newspaper on which his mother managed to get him a job, in order to save him from re-education. The narrator and Luo offer to fulfill his mission, which he cannot do himself, in exchange for new books. However, the songs they bring back to him are bawdy and, although Four-Eyes decides to publish them anyway, after having edited them, he nonetheless refuses to give them the books he had promised in exchange; they go their separate ways after the narrator, furious, violently strikes him. Luo is all the more saddened by this failure that he notices the fascination of the Little Seamstress for some chosen excerpts of Balzac's work.

Shortly after these events, Four-Eyes' mother comes to fetch her son and organizes a big party for the occasion. The narrator and Luo use this opportunity to steal the bag of books, at the suggestion of the Little Seamstress.

For about a month, taking advantage of the absence of the head of the village, the two friends devour the contents of the bag: Hugo (1802-1885), Stendhal (1783-1842), Dumas (1802-1870), Flaubert (1821-1880), etc. Jean-Christophe (1904-1912) by Romain Rolland (1866-1944) generates the enthusiasm of the narrator, while Luo remains a fond reader of Balzac, and goes each day to read extracts to the Little Seamstress.

Sometime later, the father of the young woman, a travelling tailor, comes to spend some time in the village. At his request, the narrator begins to tell him the story of *The Count of Monte-Cristo* (1845) by Alexandre Dumas, which he has read recently, over the course of nine nights. However, on the third night, the head of the village interrupts them: he accuses them of telling reactionary stories and threatens to denounce them, unless Luo, the son of a prestigious dentist, manages to heal his terribly painful tooth. The young man manages to do so with the help of the narrator and the tailor, whose sewing machine is converted into a medical machine. This scene gives the narrator, who powers the pedal of the machine, which impacts the speed of the machine, the opportunity to express his hatred towards the head of the village and to show sadism.

Shortly after, Luo is called to the bedside of his ill mother. He entrusts the care of the Little Seamstress to the narrator, but this sparks the jealousy of Luo's rivals, who end up treating him badly. Moreover, the narrator himself is forced to recognize that he has feelings for the young woman that make his role as protector hypocritical. Just as he is about to confess to her that he does not wish to come to her house any longer, she informs him that she is pregnant. Yet the Chinese regime, which forbids a woman to have children without being married, also forbids abortion. Therefore, the narrator goes to the hospital of Yong Jing to explore the possibility of an illegal abortion. He finally manages to get in touch with the gynecologist, who agrees to carry out the procedure in exchange for a book by Balzac.

The operation takes place without any problems, but three months after Luo's return, the Little Seamstress leaves the mountain without warning the two friends. It is his father who, in despair, comes to tell them the news. Surreptitiously, reading the novels by Balzac has changed the young woman from the mountain, whose main aim was to please Luo, into a woman who wishes to be desired and to become a city woman. Resolute, the Little Seamstress left after having declared that Balzac made her understand something: the beauty of a woman is a priceless treasure. Although the novel ends with these words, according to the author, the final image conveyed by the novel is the one he depicts at the beginning of the last chapter: Luo burning all the books of the bag, while the narrator accompanies this book-burning with the sounds of his violin.

CHARACTER STUDY

THE NARRATOR

Anonymous, he is one of the main characters, although he stays in the background compared to his friend Luo, definitely granting the center of the stage to his friend's love story with the Little Seamstress. Moreover, at the end of the novel, he defines himself as an onlooker.

The son of a doctor, like Luo, he is 17 when his re-education begins, the narrator is taller and stronger than his friend. He is also shier and more reasonable, although from time to time he falls prey to violent urges (for example, the time when he struck Four-eyes, or the sadism with which he behaved towards the village leader when his tooth was being treated).

Loyal where friendship is concerned, he is careful not to betray his feelings for the Little Seamstress, who Luo loves, and is deeply affected when the young woman, who he considers a friend, disappears without warning, after he has faithfully helped and supported her during her unwanted pregnancy.

A musician, passionate about *Jean-Christophe* by Romain Rolland (whose main protagonist is a musician), he hopes that his talent as a violinist will one day help him to escape from re-education.

LUO

He is the narrator's best friend. On a psychological level, he is curious and nonchalant, and has a great talent for improvisation and timing, as shown by his reaction when the villagers got suspicious of the violin, or when the miller came to pay a visit. As stated by the narrator, he has a strategic intelligence and is unbridled, generous, and fiery.

Proof of his courage and stubbornness, Luo braves the terrible vertigo he suffers from each day to go read abstracts from Balzac's work to the Little Seamstress. Pride seems to be at the origin of this process (the Little Seamstress is not "civilized" enough to be worthy of him, Part 1, Chapter 3) yet retrospectively, it becomes clear that it is the love he bears towards the young woman that prompts him to act: not only did he fall in love with her, even though she is nothing but a simple village girl, but, more strikingly, at the end of the novel he chooses to burn all the books in the bag, as they are the source of this culture which he held so high, but which caused him to lose the woman he loves. This great admirer of Balzac is therefore first and foremost a romantic.

THE TWO FRIENDS

They embody the youth that suffered unjustly from the measures dictated by the Maoist regime in the context of the Cultural Revolution as they are condemned to be re-educated, although their sole crime was being the sons of educated men fallen out of grace. They know their chances of seeing the end of their re-education period are thin.

They also symbolize a passive resistance to this attempt at bridling the intellectuals: they do not openly rebel against the regime, but indirectly defend themselves by fighting to get access to the Western books, despite the risk involved, and to spread their contents to the people who want to hear about it (the Little Seamstress, her father).

THE LITTLE SEAMSTRESS

The Little Seamstress, whose name is not given by the narrator, is the only character to be physically described in some detail: in addition to her clothes, which separate her from the other villagers (a brand new ribbon, shoes, etc.), she is set apart because of her beauty: she has a long plait, the most beautiful eyes in the whole Yong Jin district, a face whose outline is neat, almost noble, etc. Nonetheless, her remarkable beauty is that of a peasant-girl: "When she laughed I noticed an untamed quality about her eyes, which reminded me of the wild girls on our side of the mountain. Her eyes had the gleam of uncut gems, of unpolished metal" (Part 1, Chapter 3). These descriptive elements are important because it is precisely a change in physical appearance and clothing that will reflect, at the end of the story, the inner change undergone by the young woman.

Mischievous and full of laughter, she seems to be sincerely in love with Luo, whom she loves to please, as a mountain girl, until reading works by Balzac awakens her ambition to become a city girl.

THE HEAD OF THE VILLAGE

He is the only villager not to be lost in the indifferent mass of peasants. This character is a kind of symbolic figure representing the communist peasant, and expresses both through his actions and his appearances the intellectual and physical misery of the Chinese peasantry: he is dirty, disgusting (he has spots of blood in his left eye), he also used to suffer from syphilis (with everything it entails in the collective imagination).

An authoritarian man, wishing not to lose face and not to betray his ignorance (he says the violin is a toy), he is nevertheless very naïve and easily duped, as shown by the trick concerning Mozart's (German composer, 1756-1791) sonata, which reminds him of president Mao (1893-1976). His credulity is proof of his stupidity and lack of general knowledge, but also of his ideological convictions, that seem to be a true conditioning (when he hears the name Mao, his whole face softens, as though he has heard something miraculous, Part 1, Chapter 1).

The figure of the leader is the opportunity to paint a less than complimentary portrait of the Chinese communist peasantry, brutified by the regime: a total lack of opening to civilization and bourgeois culture, which is the ideal of the Chinese communist party, leads to stupidity and ignorance, making people naïve and easily manipulated.

ANALYSIS

HISTORICAL CONTEXT: THE CULTURAL REVOLUTION

The historical and political context is very important in Dai Sije's novel, which focuses on the condition of the intellectual people in the Maoist china of the 1970s, in the wake of the Cultural Revolution. Let's consider the origins of this movement.

In the 1950s, Mao launched an ambitious policy of industrial and agricultural development, called the Great Leap Forward. Led with extreme and unrealistic ideological rigor, this policy was a failure. Its effects were even catastrophic: a widespread famine caused the deaths of millions of people.

Mao was then distanced from presidency and replaced by communist leaders. To take the upper hand again, he chose to initiate a cultural reform: "Considering that the regime was tending towards revisionism [...] Mao Zedong , did not hesitate to trigger a true insurrection of the youth in the form of the Red Guards Movements, which officially started on 18th August 1966" (Mourre, M., *Le Petit Mourre. Dictionnaire de l'histoire*, Paris, Larousse/HER, 2001, p.208)[1].

This was the beginning of the Cultural Revolution, which would last until Mao's death in 1976. The Red Guards spread

---

1. Quotes taken from the original are translated by BrightSummaries.com.

the idolatrous worship of Mao and of his *Little Red Book* (a book of quotes by Mao himself) in the countryside, arriving in mass by train. They started eliminating all the revisionist functionaries of the party and the intellectuals, an exploiting class soaked up in bourgeois capitalist ideology, whose representatives and culture should both be erased. It should be noted that although Westerners mainly remember the prohibition of many Western values and culture, the traditional values, considered to belong to the exploiting classes, were also targeted: the Red Guards destroyed many temples and Buddhist statues. In fact, in the background of the ideological struggle, a political struggle took place that enabled Mao to eliminate the leaders of the communist party that were not favorable to him, and to resume his function as president of the People's Republic of China.

AN AUTOBIOGRAPHICAL STORY?

The genre of the novel might be problematic. Indeed, some elements suggest that it may be an autobiography:

- Dai Sije's parents were doctors, like those of the narrator;
- The author had also been sent, from 1971 to 1974, to a small mountain village in Sichuan, the province in which the story is set, to be re-educated;
- The narration is in the first person singular;
- It is not explicitly stated that the text is a novel.

Yet an autobiographical story implies a correspondence between the author, the narrator and the main protagonist. This is not the case here:

- The main protagonist is Luo;
- The narrator and the author do not have the same name. Even though the name of the narrator is never given, the objects represented by the three Chinese characters of his name are mentioned: a horse, a sword and a small bell, which in Chinese results in the name Ma Jian Ling.

Therefore, the novel cannot be considered an autobiography in the strict meaning of the word, as there is no total coherence between the author and the narrator. However, it is obvious that the author took his inspiration from his personal experience, namely his experience of re-education, to create this novelized fiction, which gives it the worth of a testimony, in a certain measure.

AN AUTHENTIC AND SOBER TESTIMONY

The specificity of this testimony resides in two elements. First, it lies in its authenticity. The depiction of re-education and the excesses of the regime is not focused on a specific element, but is created by small touches throughout the story of the characters, in the tiniest details of everyday life: the readers discover in turn the humiliation undergone by Luo's parents, the insalubrious conditions of the village houses, the extremely hard (the baskets that are to be carried) and dangerous (the mine) working conditions, the interdiction of Western books, the use of connections (Four-Eyes' job), etc.

The novel is also distinguished by its neutral and factual tone. As opposed to many testimonies, the sobriety of the tone used by the narrator is striking. This can be surprising at times, as the characters are seemingly passive in the face of their destinies, to which they seem to have resigned themselves. These elements play a key role in the way the novel is met by the reader:

- They contribute to its objectivity and leave the reader free to interpret. By limiting himself to the description of the facts, that narrator gives his character a neutral and objective character. The reader remains free to construct his own opinion based on the facts described;
- They embody the effects of the regime. Although the narrator distances himself from the regime, the lack of severe or outraged judgments in his testimony about what he is forced to go though can be seen as an effect of the dictatorship in place. Born into that regime, he considers what he goes through as normal and inevitable, because he does not know any different ("We were not the first to be used as guinea pigs in this grand human experiment, nor would we be the last[...]Compared with others we were not too badly off. Millions of young people had gone before us, and millions would follow." (Part 1, Chapter 1);
- The tone, defined by a sort of fatalistic realism, paradoxically managed to strengthen the reader's indignation, as the effects of the dictatorial Chinese regime are not only visible in the facts described in the novel, but also in the tone of the narrator. The reach of the dictatorship is such that rebellion and outrage are no longer natural reflexes, not only because they are constantly reined in, but also because they can be dangerous, as stated by the narrator himself after expressing his hatred: "Hearing myself utter this last sentence frightened me, as if there might

be an eavesdropper hidden somewhere in the room. Such a remark, casually dropped, could cost several years in prison".

THE PARADOXES OF RE-EDUCATION

Against the background of re-education and the Cultural Revolution, Sije's novel actually depicts not one but several (re-)educations, which overlap and function in a paradoxical way:

- The two protagonists, considered to be intellectuals, are sent to the mountains to be re-educated by poor peasants. This initiative does not seem to have any effect on them: although they share the everyday life of the peasants, they remain closed to their ideology. Moreover, it is during their stay in the mountains that they will have access to Western books for the first time, while at college, they were reading communist school books or Mao's *Little Red Book*. The Western books are truly responsible for their education, making them discover the outside world, women, love, and sex. Therefore, it is not only a cultural, but also a sentimental education, which materializes in the love story between Luo and the Little Seamstress. Thus, sending the two young people to re-education has paradoxically exactly the opposite effect: they open up to Western culture and bourgeois values, symbolized by Balzac's novels;
- The Little Seamstress is also educated by reading Balzac, which satisfies Luo who did not think her civilized enough for him. Having noticed the effect that reading abstracts

from *Father Goriot* to the young girl had on her, ("This fellow Balzac is a wizard. . . . He touched the head of this mountain girl with an invisible finger, and she was transformed, carried away in a dream", Part 2, Chapter 3) he decided that reading Balzac would make her more refined, more knowledgeable. Thus, Luo turns literature into a tool, making it the means of the indoctrination, or at least of the education of the Little Seamstress.

Consequently, it is the two young men who had been sent to the countryside to be re-educated who actually re-educated the young woman; but because he wanted her to be made deserving of his love, Luo lost her: the Balzacian re-education he undertook did not happen as he wished it. However, is it not the case that any attempt at re-educating people and turning them into something they are not is an inevitably dangerous operation?

FURTHER REFLECTION

SOME QUESTIONS TO THINK ABOUT....

- The novel is based on real historical facts. What are they? Do you know of any other works depicting a real historical framework, yet which are not historical?
- In your opinion, who is the main protagonist, the narrator or Luo? Justify your answer.
- Can this work be seen as an autobiography? Explain your answer.
- In your opinion, why does the author adopt a neutral and objective tone? What effect does this have on the reader?
- In the novel, not one, but many (re-)educations are mentioned. What are they? How are they paradoxical?
- Balzac is at the core of Dai Sije's novel. Explain the importance of this figure.
- What perspective on reading does this novel convey?
- The author chose to put specific books in the bag stolen by the two protagonists, namely by Hugo, Stendhal, Dumas, Flaubert and Roman Rolland. Do these books shed a new or explanatory light on what the characters are going through?
- In your opinion, how can the last sentence of the novel be interpreted: what is the Little Seamstress going to do in the city? Is she thinking about making a good marriage, about prostitution, or about something else entirely?

We want to hear from you!
Leave a comment on your online library
and share your favourite books on social media!

FURTHER READING

REFERENCE EDITION

- Sije, D. (2002) *Balzac and the Little Chinese Seamstress*. London: Vintage Books.

ADAPTATIONS

- *Balzac et la Petite Tailleuse chinoise*. (2002) [Film]. Dai Sijie. Dir.
  Although the book was written in French, the actors played in Chinese. The narrator, whose name is not mentioned in the novel, is called Ma in the film (in accordance with the Chinese characters mentioned in the novel).

www.brightsummaries.com

Ebook EAN: 9782806270566

Paperback EAN: 9782806275325

Legal Deposit: D/2016/12603/6

Cover: © Primento

Digital conception by Primento, the digital partner of publishers.

Printed in Great Britain
by Amazon